TWO SLEUTHS & A SWIMMING POOL

MRS. POMOLO INVESTIGATES

DONNA MUSE

Tica House
Publishing

Sweet Romance that Delights and Enchants!

PERSONAL WORD FROM THE AUTHOR

DEAREST READERS,

I'm so delighted that you have chosen one of my books to read. I have recently joined the team of writers at Tica House Publishing. Our goal is to inspire, entertain, and give you many hours of reading pleasure. Your kind words and loving readership are deeply appreciated.

Along with my fellow authors, I would like to personally invite you to sign up for updates and to become part of our **Exclusive Reader Club**—it's completely Free to Join!

Much love, Donna Muse

CLICK HERE to Join our Reader's Club and to Receive Tica House Updates!

https://cozymystery.subscribemenow.com/

CONTENTS

[1]

"How many of these people have actually *read* the *Alice* books, though?" asked George Wilson, gazing in disapproval at the crowd gathered round them. "It's been my experience that most people don't read it at all."

"It's one of the most beloved books of the Victorian era," said his lady friend of some years, Geneva Pomolo. Geneva preferred to take a more optimistic view of the reading public, in spite of all the evidence—it helped keep her sane. "People still read it."

They were gathered on Wrangler's Hill Commons—they and Geneva's housemate, Iris Reeves, a chubby, cheerful woman with streaks of gray in her frizzled hair—for a celebration of Lewis Carroll's *Alice* novels. It was May fourth, the date on which the events of *Alice in Wonderland* were supposed to take place.

To commemorate the event, the city had set up a fairground on the commons at which all sorts of *Alice*-themed events had been scheduled—a tea party, a croquet game with mallets shaped like flamingoes, a caterpillar train for children to ride on. Various costumed characters wandered amid the booths and displays; already Geneva had spotted the Queen of Hearts, the White Knight, and a pair of twins in matching schoolboy outfits who could only have been Tweedledum and Tweedledee. Many of the costumes borrowed more from the aesthetic of the recent film adaptations than from John Tenniel's original illustrations, a fact which had occasioned George's disapproving remark.

"Personally, I don't care whether they've read the book or not," said Iris, patting her belly with a rueful air. "I would like to find one vendor in this place who sells decent food."

But for the moment, decent food seemed out of the question. Since entering the commons, they had seen vendors selling jam tarts, treacle, bread and butter, and one bright young woman in a purple striped hat hawking oysters on the half-shell—"which I certainly won't be eating," said Geneva, remembering the fate of the oysters in the poem. "You all can eat what you like."

"No oysters for me," said Iris sadly. "Growing up in South Carolina, I once ate canned oysters during a hurricane when we ran out of food. Made me sick for three days."

Geneva wondered idly whether Iris had any memories of South Carolina that weren't traumatic. "Well, no one is making you eat them now."

"Too right," said Iris, attempting to see over the head of a man dressed like Bill the Lizard. "I'd give anything right now for a decent taco."

"On the map, they gave us at the entrance," said George, waving a pamphlet round, "there's a stand called 'the Dodo's Tacos.' We could try that."

"Don't believe it," said Geneva, a little irritably. "The vendors keep switching places, I guess because they thought it would be in the spirit of the books to make things confusing and frustrating."

"You know what?" said Iris. "I respect it."

Iris kept walking and the others followed. The sun was bearing down, making the back of Geneva's neck wet and sticky. They passed two girls of about seven or eight, one of them wearing a Cheshire Cat t-shirt, arguing over a water bottle. The girls seemed to have gotten separated from their parents, but they didn't look particularly fussed about it.

A bit further on, stood a booth where a woman was selling prints of illustrations from the books and wall hangings with quotes that were *not* from the books, although they claimed to be. ("Everyone's a little bit insane," read one, allegedly spoken by the Cat.) Twenty yards further on, a couple of women were, somewhat futilely, attempting to organize a caucus race for children under the age of twelve. The children were running frenziedly in all directions while the women blew their whistles with a helpless air.

"This is a mess, honestly," said Iris, patting her increasingly frizzy hair, "and the heat isn't helping. Why couldn't they have done this in November?"

"November isn't when the events of *Through the Looking-Glass* take place," said George brightly. "It says so on the pamphlet."

"I don't trust that pamphlet," said Iris, scowling. "And I don't have a good feeling about this place if we're being honest. Two thousand people all running amuck in the hot sun... minimal police presence... seems like a recipe for trouble, doesn't it?"

"You worry too much," said Geneva.

Iris raised a skeptical brow. "When have you ever worried *enough*?"

They emerged from the little warren of vendors and booths into an open grassy place near the lake, at the front of which stood a makeshift stage with five or six rows of metal folding chairs, such as one might see at a church potluck, laid before it. Most of the chairs were empty; but a man in a rumpled tweed coat and horn-rimmed glasses stood at a lectern on the stage, flanked on either side by black-and-white photographs of Lewis Carroll in his youth.

"A reader of the *Alice* books who's never been to Oxford," he was saying, shuffling his papers importantly, "might not grasp just how much the books are indebted to the landscape of the place. Carroll was writing about a world that he *knew*—and knew very well. Morton Cohen, in his seminal biography, calls Wonderland a funhouse-mirror version of the ancient university town: the treacle well and the sheep shop and the lilies were all recognizable Oxfordian landmarks; the royal crests bore the Lion and the Unicorn; there are several theories as to the origin of the Cheshire Cat..."

"He is about to put me to sleep," said Iris, actually yawning. "Let's get going; I have a sudden, inexplicable craving for hot-cross buns."

"No, wait," said Geneva, feeling weirdly transfixed. "I want to hear this."

Iris muttered something that sounded like "English teachers," but remained standing in place.

"Because Carroll was such a meticulous diary-keeper, we know precisely when and where the germ of the story that would become *Alice* first came to him. On July 3, 1862, he and his friend Robinson Duckworth went on a rainy excursion with the three young daughters of Henry Liddell, Dean of Christchurch—one of whom, Alice, was his particular favorite. As the whole party got thoroughly drenched, they decided to try again the next day. This day it was sunny. They took a boat out on the river; and, seeing that the girls were getting sleepy and bored—"

Iris stifled another yawn.

"... Carroll spontaneously started making up a story. A story about a girl by the name of Alice, who follows a white rabbit down a rabbit hole into a strange and chaotic realm. The girls loved it so much that they encouraged him to write it down, which Carroll did with some reluctance. After the first two thousand copies of the printed edition had to be recalled and destroyed because of a problem with the illustrations, he paid out of pocket to have it reprinted, writing in a letter to a friend that he was losing huge sums of money."

The speaker, who all this while had been staring rigidly and attentively at his notes, now glanced up at the dwindling audience. "Carroll couldn't have imagined how lucrative his little book would become. At an auction in Indianapolis in

2016, a long-time resident of Wrangler's Hill bought a first edition copy of *Alice* for three million dollars."

George let out a low whistle. "What I wouldn't give to see that."

"Three million?" said Geneva. "Who in Wrangler's Hill has that kind of money?"

They went on talking about the lecture in excited tones as they made their way back to Iris's car. Iris thought it an egregious waste of money to pay millions for a book that was freely available online. George told her she was missing the point: "It's the ownership of the thing," he said quietly. "Just knowing that you owned something rare and precious."

"I have a corgi at home," Iris pointed out. "And she already costs me a fortune."

"I'm not sure I could ever bring myself to spend the money," said Geneva, "not when there are so many starving kids and underfunded public schools. But I get the impulse. I get it."

George veered a little way off the sidewalk to let a small girl, painted to resemble the Red Queen, skate past them. "Whoever it was, I hope she or he is keeping it under lock and key. A treasure of that magnitude must be a magnet for burglars."

"And grifters," said Geneva. She had read too many stories of rich, widowed women who had been charmed out of their immense fortunes by silver-tongued gentlemen with seemingly humble aspirations and a knack for flattery. "Always the same story: 'You can trust me, miss, I'm one of the good ones, not like those other men who would just as soon rob you blind...' Then she wakes up one morning, about three weeks after the wedding, and he's managing her whole estate and business, and she no longer has any say over her own finances. And if she protests, she risks finding herself at the bottom of a river, or pushed down the stairs—"

"Maybe I *don't* want to be rich," said Iris, patting her voluminous hair. "I have enough problems."

"Rich or poor," said Geneva sagely, "we all have our troubles."

"I'd be scared that I couldn't trust whomever I was dating." Iris retrieved her keys from her pants pocket. "If I was a rich heiress with a fortune of untold millions, I would simply keep that a secret from prospective suitors. I'm sure the revelation would come as a nice surprise to the person I chose to marry —who had fallen in love with my sparkling wit and lively personality."

"Is this your way of telling us you're an heiress?" George asked.

"Don't you wish?" Iris laughed. "If I was, do you think I would be living in that beat-up old house?"

"I think it's a very fine house—" said Geneva, but she was interrupted by the sudden appearance of an ugly old woman in a flowing red robe, who was shambling hastily toward them from across the crowded parking lot.

She was, thought Geneva, quite the ugliest woman she had ever seen. She wore a tightly laced dress and a scarlet head-dress, with a veil only partially concealing her haggard, toothless face. In the place where her eyebrows ought to have been, there was no hair, only a pair of what looked like scorch marks roughly the shape and length of a caterpillar, as if she had burned them off her face with a lighter. In one hand she carried a bright yellow daffodil, which she held out, as she approached, as if offering it to them.

Although they had by now reached the car, the three friends were so transfixed by the hideousness of the figure they made no attempt to get in. It was as though a spell had fallen over them, which they were powerless to dispel. The woman signaled with her hands to suggest she wanted to address them; given the haste with which she ran forward, nearly tripping over her own skirts, it was obviously a matter of some urgency.

By now, Geneva and Iris were famous enough locally that it wouldn't have been at all surprising if she had recognized them on the commons. More than once at church, Geneva had been approached by some disgruntled parishioner whose husband had suddenly vanished, taking all her money, or one who suspected her next-door neighbors of being involved in some criminal ring, and wanted her to investigate. So it came as some surprise when the mysterious woman placed the daffodil in George's hands, closing his fingers over the stem, and said, "Are you George Wilson?"

George blinked rapidly, as if no one had ever spoken his name before. "Yes?" he replied.

"The George Wilson, I'm to understand, who lives at—" and here she gave his exact address, just as if she was reading it.

"Yes, that's me," said George, a little warily.

"I'm sorry, did you need something?" said Geneva, feeling instinctively protective.

The woman acted as though she hadn't heard her. "George, I've something I need to tell you, and I need you to listen very carefully. There are people who don't want me to say what I'm about to say—who would do terrible things if they knew what secret I was about to betray."

Surely, Geneva felt, this was some kind of prank, inflicted on the guileless George. But George looked utterly rapt. "Do go on," he said low.

"You had a relationship with a woman some thirty years ago," said the woman, slowly and clearly. "Out of that union, short-lived though it was, came a daughter—"

"I'm sorry, a *what?*" cried Iris.

"A daughter who is now fully grown. She hasn't moved far. She still lives in the Wrangler's Hill area. It would be a betrayal of her confidence, and the confidence of others, if I were to say anymore. But George, know this: your little girl is in terrible danger. She's in league with people who aren't looking after her best interests. Criminals and scammers and cutthroats. She's looking for a way out, but she may never find it. You need to find her. You need to save her. Right now, the whole future course of her life may depend on you."

George stood stone-still, looking as though he had about a million questions. "Well, if that's all," said Geneva, feeling distinctly affronted, "I suppose you'll be going now..."

The woman nodded from beneath her scarlet headdress, then turned to leave.

"Honestly, the pranks these women play," said Geneva when she had gone. "You were never in a relationship before we started going out, were you, George?"

George gazed at his hands. "No, I... I had a reputation for being something of a ladies' man back in my youth. They called me 'the Poet,' because I was so gangly and depressed, and I scribbled bad verses at four in the morning. Every woman at Purdue wanted to feed me soup and tuck me into bed."

"But you had never so much as *kissed* a woman," said Geneva. "You were so shy and prim."

George was silent.

"There was a woman," he said at last, after a lengthy pause. "Never mind her real name—I call her Irene, as in Irene Adler."

He glanced at Geneva to make sure she had gotten the reference; she had.

"We spent a blissful ten months together during my junior and senior years of college. They were possibly the happiest ten months of my life. Irene was so sharp—a poet, a songwriter, a lover of Dickens. On summer days, we would go out rowing and she would play her guitar on the water. There was one day—I still remember it so well, all these years later—we visited the botanical gardens. Afterward we spent an hour or two at sunset walking along the river, at the end of which she handed me—this."

He opened his palm to reveal the daffodil.

"It became our special flower," he said, "more precious than the rose. She gave me a vase-full for my birthday. I woke one morning to find they had all withered. I went over to her house, and she had gone—cleared out in the night, leaving only a note. Said she was sorry, but she had to move on. I spent a month looking for her but never found her. Up until this moment, I wasn't even sure she was still alive."

$$[\ 2\ ]$$

An uneasy silence hung over the station wagon most of the way to Whataburger.

"Georgie, dear," said Geneva, as they were sitting in the mostly empty restaurant, "you've barely touched your Honey Butter Chicken Biscuit."

George gazed sullenly down at his chicken biscuit. The chicken part was too crisp, and the biscuit part was too soggy. "I'm not feeling particularly hungry. But I hate seeing food go to waste. I think I'll pack this up and take it home to eat later."

"You sure you don't have something on your mind?" asked Iris, who had overloaded her Whataburger with ketchup so that the ketchup was spilling over onto her tray. "Anything you wanna talk about?"

"Not particularly," said George weakly.

The group was silent for a moment. It seemed clear that everyone else at the table had something they very much wanted to discuss.

"I was thinking of finding a halfway-decent adaptation of *Alice in Wonderland* to watch when we're eating dinner tonight," said George, who had been scrolling through his phone all this while. "'Halfway decent' narrows it down considerably. Among the Victorians I follow, the most popular choices seem to be the black-and-white BBC adaptation from the 1960s or the TV miniseries from the—"

"George," said Geneva, in a warning tone.

"... mid-1980s," said George limply. "The one from the sixties is interesting because the characters don't even bother to wear costumes. They're more or less ordinary British men and women with strange manners of speech whom Alice meets as she wanders across a university campus. It's somehow both mundane and trippy. There's also a version of *Through the Looking Glass* from the seventies starring a young Sarah Sutton—"

"George," said Geneva, a little more sternly.

George hung his head. "Oh, all right. I suppose we'll have to discuss it eventually, so we may as well get it out of the way now."

"Very sensibly put," said Geneva, taking a small sip of her soft drink. "It would behoove us to face the fact that somewhere in Indiana you may very well have a child."

"You say child as if she wouldn't already be fully grown," George replied. "It's like that episode of *Doctor Who* where the fish people steal some of the Doctor's DNA and create a twenty-something daughter."

"Yes, that's exactly what it's like," said Geneva sarcastically. "And do you have any particular feelings on the subject? I can't imagine what I would be feeling if I had just learned I was a mother, but I don't think I would be googling *Alice in Wonderland* adaptations."

George shoved his phone down into his pants pocket, looking a little embarrassed.

"Well, I mean, it doesn't sound very likely, does it?" he said, with a great deal more feeling than he had yet shown. "I think it was—if not a prank—then maybe a scam of some sort. The woman has heard of us, and she knows you have a thriving business working as a private investigator, and she thought she could wring some money out of you."

Geneva nodded. "Yes, that was my first thought. Nine times out of ten you can ignore the mysterious woman and go about your day."

"But the daffodil—" said Iris.

"But the daffodil," said Geneva. "George, how do you explain that?"

George seemed to have been considering this for some time. "It's one of those thingummies—what do they call it—cold reading? The woman hands you a flower and hopes that it means something to you, which, most people have important memories associated with flowers. I bet she's handed out flowers to hundreds of people, all with some harebrained story about a lost child."

Geneva sat back in her seat and slapped the table lightly, looking impressed.

"So you *do* listen to me sometimes," she said proudly. "When we first met, you were the most credulous, gullible, super-stitious—"

"An idiot, I know," said George, with a touch of resentment. "No need to go rubbing it in."

"But if I've taught you nothing else in our years together, it's how to recognize the mind games of scammers and grifters and con artists. Someday soon, I'll be able to send you to the grocers' without having to worry that you'll come home with a bag of magic beans."

"Leave me in charge of the groceries for now, please," said Iris, beginning to consolidate all their trash. "So you think it was all lies, then?"

"No, not at all," said Geneva, to the surprise of all parties.

Iris gave her a stony glare. "But you just said—"

"I think it's wise to exercise caution. But in this case, I think we have good reason to suspect the old woman was telling the truth. At the very least, we ought to look into it."

"And just how do you propose to do that?" Iris asked.

Geneva examined her nails, thinking. "Well, it would help if she had given us a number, or any sort of contact info. In the absence of that, there are courthouse records that we could request, birth and adoption papers—"

At this George threw up his hands. "You can do whatever you like," he said with sudden vehemence, "but please, I'm begging you, leave me out of it."

The two women stared at him, dumbstruck.

"Are you not remotely curious?" asked Iris.

"If you have a daughter," said Geneva, "wouldn't you like to meet her?"

"No, and no," said George, looking in every direction but theirs. "If the woman spoke true, and we still don't know if she did, then it's none of my business. That little girl is living her life. She doesn't need any interference from me. If she wanted to meet me, she'd have met me by now."

He had risen slightly while speaking, but now slid down again into his booth. Geneva regarded him silently, sensing there was some deeper sentiment at work he was keen to conceal, if he even knew it was there.

"Well, look, I don't want this to turn into a whole thing," she said, "but if she's been looking for you, maybe this is her way of telling you. Maybe she sent that woman."

"She shouldn't have," said George plainly. "Either find me yourself or don't bother."

One of the more exasperating things about dating George was how prickly he could get when his feelings were injured—which wasn't hard to do, he was so sensitive. When he got in these moods, Geneva had learned to pull back a little so as not to escalate the flare-up into a full-blown fight.

"George may or may not have a daughter... just something to keep in mind, I guess." Somehow the meal had turned into a semi-formal meeting; it made her feel like she was back in high school, presiding over the debate club. "Second order of business: I'd love to find whoever owns that first-edition copy of *Alice in Wonderland.*"

"Why?" said Iris, picking off the last of her fries. "Are they in trouble?"

"I don't know. I have an odd feeling they might be," said Geneva, "but I don't know that for sure. In general, I think it's a good idea to be cognizant of all the people living in our area who have two or three million dollars to blow on so-called frivolous things."

"I'd like to see it, personally," said George, looking relieved at the change of subject.

"Yes, and there's that." Geneva drummed her nails on the sticky tabletop. "I feel a sense of curiosity about this person— man or woman, and I feel quite certain it's a woman—"

George harrumphed indignantly. "It could be a man," he said.

"Regardless, I'd like to meet the sort of person who would willingly spend the GDP of a lesser European monarchy on a children's book from the Victorian era. I think that person and I would have things to talk about. I think we might even be bosom friends."

"Do the rich have anything to say to us?" asked Iris skeptically. "In general, I think they just want to be left alone with their toys."

Geneva was adamant, though. "No, I've got a feeling about her. I do. It means we're not the only people in this backwater town with good taste."

Iris pursed her lips. "And what if she accuses you of trying to steal her precious book and kicks you to the curb?"

Geneva motioned to herself with a gesture of feigned surprise. "Who, me? Little old lady English teacher from the sticks?"

"All I'm saying," said Iris, rising from the table and grabbing their trays, "is you don't know what you're getting into. The rich aren't like us. They're trouble. I've dated enough of them to know."

Geneva spent most of the next several days attempting to locate the mysterious woman who had bought the *Alice* book at auction. A scan of all the items pertaining to the auction written up in the local papers yielded not one mention of her name, which she had evidently intended to be kept private. Finally in desperation, Geneva phoned her liaison at the Wrangler's Hill Police Department, Gerry Nelson, who listened as well as he could—the building had recently flooded, and he was attempting to dry out his carpet on the cheap with a large fan, which was both ineffective and loud.

"As an English teacher and a former member of the Victorian Society of Wrangler's Hill," said Geneva, "I feel like I ought to know—I'm sorry, would you mind turning that down?"

"Sorry, can't hear you," said Gerry, "let me go out into the hall." She could hear a door closing behind him as the noise lessened. "What were you saying?"

Geneva repeated what she had said about being a member of the Victorian Society. "I have a suspicion that I may have met this woman—though how she never mentioned owning such a rare gem is a mystery."

"Yes, I can't imagine someone not wanting to divulge their personal transactions," said Gerry dryly. "The thing you have to understand is that Victorians are a lot more common than you think. I know you lot like to think you're special, but there are probably hundreds of people wearing bowler hats and whatnot in a town this size."

"That's a lot of codswallop," said Geneva coldly.

"Well, I can't make you believe what you don't want to believe." In the background, the fan still hummed, faintly. "But compared to just about any other era in history—I mean, we have the annual Lewis Carroll festival in May, the Dickens Christmas Jamboree in December—"

This was true; the annual Dickens event in downtown Wrangler's Hill was one of the most beloved events on the municipal calendar. "Your point being?" said Geneva.

"Don't make assumptions," said Gerry. "It may not be who you think."

From the tone of his voice, it sounded like Gerry knew more than he was letting on.

"Do *you* know this person?"

Gerry made a disgruntled noise, like a cat clearing its throat. "Look, there was a whole to-do when this book was bought at auction. The lady wanted twenty-four/seven security stationed around her house to protect against thieves. I told her she could hire private mercenaries if that was her concern—"

"Did she?"

"*We're* not out there guarding the place, so I assume she did." Gerry gave a muffled cough. "Sorry... mildew. Honestly this whole building probably needs to be razed and rebuilt, but we don't have that kind of—"

"And I'm guessing you weren't particularly worried about the theft of a book?"

Gerry scoffed, as if to say, "Should I have been?" Aloud he said, "I think the probability of someone wanting a 150-year-old book enough to break into a heavily fortified manor in West Wrangler's Hill is—"

"You just said there were hundreds of us," said Geneva, quietly noting the location of the house, and that it was indeed a woman buyer.

"Yeah, but Victorians aren't exactly known for being law-breakers."

"Still, that kind of money... it could be sold on the black market for a pretty sum."

"Are *you* planning to steal it?"

There was a silence in which Geneva elegantly signaled her contempt for the question.

"Listen, the book will be fine," said Gerry, after a pause. "I told Myrna, 'Just buy yourself a small safe for your bedroom or office and keep the book in the safe. If a determined thief manages to get past your state-of-the-art home security system, they'll have a world of trouble trying to open that safe, and frankly I'm not sure it would be worth the trouble.' She stopped calling me shortly after that, but I hope it helped."

"What you've just said was incredibly helpful," said Geneva, jotting a note in her memorandum book. "More than I think you realize."

And she hung up before he had a chance to respond.

A few minutes' googling yielded one millionaire living in the West End named Myrna Nettles, an eighty-two-year-old widow who was a prominent member of the local Episcopalian church and had been featured in various *Bugle* pieces over the years for her involvement in youth retreats, bake sales, and 4-H Club. Having been raised in the slums and taken over management of her husband's rental empire after his death, Mrs. Nettles had the rare ability—so seldom accessible to those born wealthy—of being able to appreciate her good fortune.

In the most recent news story, dated the previous December, she had donated one million dollars to an inner-city high school for the repair of its library—with the lone stipulation that a portion of the funds be used to buy classic novels.

"When I was a little girl growing up in Appalachia," the *Bugle* quoted her as saying, "it was the heroines of classic literature who showed me all I was capable of becoming. Jo March, Anne of Green Gables, Jane Eyre, Alice... I want the little girls of today to read those books and know there's no limit to the dreams they can dream."

A black-and-white photo accompanying the piece showed her kneeling at the back of the library, surrounded by beaming tweens in braces and pigtails. She looked no older than sixty in her platinum-blonde wig, form-hugging green satin dress and maroon sweater embroidered with a worm reading a stack of novels. "Don't bug me, I'm reading." the shirt read.

This all seemed specially calibrated to tug at Geneva's heart. In scarcely any time at all, she had found Myrna's granddaughter, Abigail, on social media and sent her a message expressing her admiration for her grandmother — and the hope that she might connect them. Geneva didn't think it wise to mention her interest in the book as yet, because she didn't want Myrna to suspect her (as she surely might) of wanting to steal it.

Messaging Abigail in this manner was a gamble, for half the time when Geneva messaged a stranger she got no response, and almost half the time the response was very nasty. But Abigail replied on the next morning—with surprising speed and civility—to say she had passed the message along to her grandmother, who would be delighted to host her and her friends at her home on the following Saturday.

"She's having a pool party for some of the kids at church on Sunday after brunch," said Abigail, "so we'll be setting up for that. You're welcome to drop in around noon or one—I'll have some snacks and refreshments laid out and feel free to help yourselves. Mamaw never tires of company—I think she gets a little lonely living up in this great big house by herself, so she's always inviting people over if she knows them from church or through a friend. She's followed your career in the paper with great interest, so of course she's eager to have you over and 'pick the brain of the great detective,' as she put it."

"What's all this guff? 'Brain of the great detective?'" said Iris, incredulous. "She makes you sound like Hercule Poirot."

"I'm afraid she'll be terribly disappointed," said Geneva, typing out a message to let her know they would be coming. "Most of our cases were solved by being in the right place at the right time, or what I can only call a benevolent providence. And the thing about luck is that it eventually runs out."

"Let's hope it doesn't run out quite yet," said Iris, examining her hair in the mirror. "I've got a date on the Sunday after next, and death would be a terrible inconvenience."

[3]

Geneva and Iris left the house at around eleven on Saturday morning and met up with George for a late breakfast at the Omeletree. George was still feeling sullen about the events on the commons the previous weekend and huffed discontentedly whenever the subject was broached (which Iris had lately made a habit of doing—"it's good for him to be reminded that he has family out there," she said to Geneva).

The meal was interrupted, just once, by a woman in her sixties with strawberry blonde hair and slightly too much mascara. She wore a pair of faded jeans and a white t-shirt featuring a picture of Loretta Lynn which said, "Proud to be a coal-miner's daughter." She approached the table with an air of timidity, hanging back just enough to signal she wanted to speak but was still working up the courage.

Finally, Geneva, who had been finishing off a bowl of pineapple chunks and was feeling frankly annoyed by the woman's attentions, turned to her and said, "Do you need something?"

Having been thus acknowledged, like a Persian subject being shown the royal scepter, the woman perked up a bit and stepped forward with both hands in her back pockets.

"So sorry for bothering y'all," she said in a Southern drawl. "I'm a great admirer of yours and I was wonderin'—"

She reached behind her and produced, seemingly from thin air, a tangerine-colored three-ring binder.

"I have a scrapbook where I collect the signatures of every celebrity who comes through Wrangler's Hill—you wouldn't believe how many there have been lately—I saw Willem Dafoe at the Seven Swine last year and he hissed at me like a possum—"

"Sure, I'll sign it," said Geneva, unclasping her handbag and digging around for a pen. But to her surprise the woman pulled the book away and said:

"Oh, begging your pardon, I wasn't talking to you. I don't even know who you are. I was rather hoping that George—"

Geneva's pen fell to the table with a clatter. Iris turned astonished eyes on George, who coughed into his hand and mumbled something about having never had the honor.

"I'm sorry," said Geneva, recovering her wounded pride, "how do you know George?"

"Oh, all the ladies know George," said the lady, laughing an odd, simpering laugh. "When we was in our teens he used to sit out by the river sketching in his little books... me and my friends would dare each other to go over and say hello, and of course he was so wrapped up in his sketches and poetry and whatnot that he hardly noticed us." Her expression turned suddenly cold and forbidding. "You wouldn't happen to be married to one of these ladies, would you?"

"He's in a relationship," said Geneva, drawing herself to her full height, "with me."

"Well." She inserted a surprising amount of contempt into this single syllable. "It's a mystery to me how you never married, George. I knew so many girls who was willing..."

Just then a tall, reedy man with a narrow, beaky face like a falcon's, wearing a trucker's hat and a Desert Storm shirt, came striding up behind her.

"Fancy," he said sternly. "How often do I have to warn you—can't even step into the restroom for three seconds—"

"They're not movie stars, Jeb," said Fancy, who seemed to have had this discussion before. "I knew George here in high school. You've no idea what it's like seeing a friend from the old days—somewhere in my bureau I still have all the love letters I wrote to you but never sent—"

George looked as though he would like to have seen those letters but kept silent on a warning look from Geneva. Jeb, looking equally less than enthralled by the direction of the conversation, grabbed Fancy by the shoulders and steered her away from the table.

"Here's what I don't get," said George when they had gone. "If they secretly all loved me as a boy, why didn't they say anything then? Why wait forty years?"

"Probably felt you were already taken," said Iris, glaring with ill-disguised contempt at the retreating figure. "Most folks aren't going to interfere if they imagine you're already dating someone and happy."

Geneva said nothing, though her mental gears were turning. If that woman had known George at the time he was dating Irene, then perhaps—? But no, she couldn't entertain the idea, not now; it would upset him too much.

Bandersnatch Manor was a 750-acre estate girded on its eastern borders by game preserves in which, as they came up the drive, Geneva glimpsed the horns of stag and a cluster of white-tailed fawns. The drive threaded for about three quarters of a mile through groves of Douglas firs and pines and wide-spreading sugar maples ostentatiously showing off their spring finery. Somewhat to their surprise, a modest suburban home stood at the end of the drive, fronted by a Victorian wraparound porch in the shade of which a young woman was seated sipping what looked to be raspberry lemonade from a mason jar and fanning herself with the laconic air of a Southern belle on a summer's day. She wore a knee-length canary-yellow skirt, pinned-up hair and cat's-eye glasses. Her outfit reminded Geneva instantly of the librarians she had known growing up in Tacoma.

"Do young people still dress like that?" she said low as they approached the house.

"Yeah, there's this trend among the youths called 'dark academia,'" said Iris, bringing the car to a stop. "It's a whole thing online."

As they emerged from the car, Geneva could see the house was only one of five or six buildings that dotted the estate, most of them standing further back at the base of the hill or half-hidden amid the pines. The place had the air of a retreat center with its uniformed staff patrolling the grounds and smoke rising in cheerful puffs from the gamekeeper's cabin. The young woman rose to greet them, saying in a loud voice, "Mamaw's getting ready, but she'll be thrilled to know you're here. Do come inside, won't you—I ran to the store this morning and bought a snack tray with crackers and carrots and cauliflowers and all kinds of cheeses..."

She went on talking effervescently as they entered the house, Geneva only half-listening. Whatever the papers might say, she acted like someone who rarely had guests and was desperate to win their approval.

"I'm Abby," she said, "but you probably already guessed that. I'm working on getting my PhD on 'Charles Dickens and the Metropolis,' which I've been told is too broad a topic—would you believe it? I did four years at a state school and hated it. I work as a teacher's assistant which Mamaw says I don't need to do, that we have money enough and to spare, but I think it's good discipline. Someday I may have to work, and I'm trying to build up a tolerance for it..."

"Your mamaw must be enormously wealthy," said Iris. They had entered a densely furnished sitting room whose walls were lined with the heads of deer and elk, their faces frozen in varying states of confusion and disbelief. "This estate is roughly the size of the Vatican."

Abby laughed lightly; Geneva thought she heard a touch of nervousness in it.

"Yes, we've been very blessed. Grandpa had a great head for business and investment. Me, I've never been particularly good with money or numbers. Mamaw is planning to leave me the estate after she dies—she's eighty-two, but we're hoping it won't be for a while yet. I told her I've got no idea how to run a place like this, much less how to manage all that money."

"It's all in having the right advisors," said Geneva sagely.

"I read somewhere about the Beatles," said George, speaking up for the first time, "that after their manager Brian Epstein died, they lost millions because they were trying to run the band themselves, and they didn't know how to properly invest all the money they were raking in. It was a bit like losing their own father."

The door opened and a young man wearing a shirt of billowy white linen and a black leather vest entered the room.

"Abigail, are you bothering these poor folks?" He was carrying a plate of grapes, crackers, figs and slices of summer sausage, none of which he offered to the assembled guests. "And you wonder why so many of our friends decline to pay us a second visit."

"How many times must I ask you not to call me *Abigail*—" said Abby. Then, seeming to remember they had guests, she said, "This is my fiancé, Bud Henderson. Grandpa intro-duced us—they were working together—"

"He had a strict rule against anyone under his employ dating you," said Bud with a smug smile. Geneva thought she discerned a whiff of alcohol on his breath. "The second he was in the ground, I asked her to marry me."

"As I recall, you were ecstatic when you learned the news of his death," said Abby. "The closest thing I had to a father—"

"Once again, you completely misread my intentions." Bud set the plate down on a granite counter and reached for a glass bottle of Jack Daniels. "I wasn't rejoicing over the circum-stances of his death—I was delighted by the fact that the one obstacle to our union had finally been eliminated."

"All the same," said Abby, seeming to draw courage from the presence of others, "I don't consider my grandfather an 'obstacle.'"

Bud rolled his eyes. "I understand your having a sentimental attachment to the old man—he raised you after your mother's death—"

"I'm sorry *you* never had family that loved you."

Bud looked, momentarily, like he had been struck in the face; but he quickly recovered himself. "It's a blessing, really. Not having eyes clouded by familial ties, I can see things from an unbiased perspective."

"Is that not, in itself, a subjective framework?" said Geneva.

Bud looked faintly surprised, as if he had only just noticed her standing there. He gave her a once-over and frowned. She had the impression he had taken her in at a glance and decided he didn't like her.

"Abby, if these are your new friends, I can't say I approve," he said snidely. "Are all women this contradictory?"

"Other people are allowed to state their opinions," said Abby (rather gently, Geneva thought). "If you didn't insist on picking fights with everyone who comes through those doors—"

"I'm sorry," said Iris, "you said y'all are *engaged?*"

[4]

THERE WAS a silence in which Geneva stared at her partner in disbelief. Bud, however, didn't seem bothered by the question. Pouring himself another glass, he said, "Yes, and we love each other dearly. Abby and I are soul mates—I'm probably the only man in the world who truly *gets* her, and vice versa. We have a sparkling intellectual chemistry which is rare even in happily married couples."

Abby sat silently, staring at the backs of her hands as he said this.

"We're very fortunate to have found each other," he added. "When Roy first hired me, she was dating the most irritating young man—one of those tweed-suited professor types. I'd enter the coffee shop and find them seated together, hunched over a volume of poetry, tears running down Abigail's face. A stint in the military would have done the boy good. He had majored in English literature at university and acquired fifty thousand in debt—I think it made him soft..."

He strode over to the divan on which Abby was seated and placed an affectionate hand on her shoulder. "I think she's happier now. She has a lot of frankly asinine ideas about faith and politics, but we're working on that—it's been a pleasure trying to disabuse her of some of her more naïve ideas about the world and how it works."

Geneva didn't like the tone in which he was speaking; though outwardly genial, there was a hint of menace in it.

"Yes, I suppose you're right," said Abby. "I did grow up believing a lot of stupid things—being raised by a woman in her sixties will do that—"

"And a very privileged old man, with no conception of the struggles of the working class," Bud said. "And a misplaced loyalty to some primitive religion peddling fairy-tales about the sweet bye-and-bye—"

"I don't see what's wrong with that," said Geneva, rather sharply.

Bud gave her a nasty smile of condescension. "No," he said, "I don't suppose you would. But before we could get married, I knew she would have to undergo some re-education—otherwise we would be continually at each other's throats—"

"And we can't have that," said Abby, a little too cheerfully. "People who are soul mates can't be constantly fighting—not when they have the mysterious connection that we have—"

"The sort of connection that almost makes you believe in a higher power," said Bud, looking faintly pleased. "Before I met Abigail, life held no meaning. I stood on the Pierpont Bridge on a spring day and contemplated jumping into the river and ending my wretched existence. Abby's re-education has given me something to live for. If I can take this simple, pious girl and bring her into the twenty-first century—"

"Bud, not everyone *wants* to live in the twenty-first century," came a woman's voice from behind him, and Myrna Nettles entered the room. "Some of us would prefer a gentler era, with no epidemics or nuclear weapons."

"An era with smallpox, and diphtheria, and sewers, and smog, where you had about a fifty / fifty chance of surviving to your first birthday," Bud replied.

"If I had a time machine," said Myrna, seating herself on the divan next to Abby, and looking, thought Geneva, like the White Queen with her grey dress and coiffed hair and sad, sad eyes—"if I had a time machine, I think I would go back to the Victorian era and live in Oxford, and befriend Reverend Dodgson and insinuate my way into his circle of acquaintance."

("Who's Reverend Dodgson?" Iris whispered.

"That's Lewis Carroll's real name," said George.)

"Well, I don't think you'd survive long there." Bud looked thrilled that a new sparring partner had entered the room. "None of the Brontë siblings lived to the age of forty—they were all drinking poisoned graveyard water—"

"They lived in the country," said Myrna. "Reverend Dodgson lived to a ripe old age, and so did Mr. Dickens."

"I suppose it was easier if you had money," said Geneva, feeling like she had wandered into a Victorian melodrama. "Same as now."

"Yes, I'm very fortunate to have grown up in America," said Myrna philosophically. "And to have married Roy at a young age, back when his business was first taking off. We didn't have a lot of money back then, but I could see his drive and ambition. He had the energy and resolve of a Dickens."

"And look where it got him," said Bud, a little tipsily. "'Into the darkness they go, the wise, the lovely—'"

"Edna St. Vincent Millay," said George. "I thought you hated poetry."

Bud winced. "I've picked up bits and pieces—you have to, if you hope to impress the ladies—"

George turned the two women his best "I told you so" face.

"Mrs. Nettles," said Geneva, "I hope you won't think us too forward, but I'm a lifelong lover of Lewis Carroll—"

"Isn't he magical?" moaned Myrna. "He had an effortless whimsy that most writers of fantasy today could never hope to capture—I've only known that kind of magic one other time in my life, when I heard *Sgt. Peppers'* for the first time in 1967."

"Lewis Carroll was John Lennon's favorite author," George pointed out.

"Yes, I suppose he would have to have been." Myrna nodded sleepily. "They were genius enough to recapture that magic— a magic that has eluded anyone who ever tried to film the books."

She shut her eyes, falling silent for so long that Geneva began to wonder if she had fallen asleep. Despite the surface veneer of politesse, the room was charged with an electric tension. Bud and Abby were barely speaking, although Bud kept glancing at her sideways as he paced in front of the hearth like a panther. He seemed to resent the presence of the three visitors, as if they were inhibiting him from speaking what- ever was on his mind. All this seemed to have passed over the graying and untroubled head of Myrna, who seemed to prefer to treat quarrels between her loved ones as though they weren't happening.

"Well, perhaps we had better be going—" said Iris, but just then Myrna opened her eyes again.

"... and I've tried to instill in Abby a love of Victorian literature," she said, blinking rapidly two or three times like the Dormouse at the Hatter's tea party. "Roy tried to discourage her from getting her degree in English—said there was no place for it in today's world—"

"That's the trouble with today's world," said Abby.

"Maybe the old man had a point," said Bud, leering horribly. "What has literature ever done for you lot, other than to make you millions of dollars poorer?"

"Millions of dollars?" said Geneva, feigning surprise. "Granted it's been a hot minute since I attended school—"

"He doesn't mean tuition," said Abby, reaching into her purse and pulling out a pair of knitting needles and some purple yarn. "Mamaw bought a book at auction a few years back—"

"Oh, don't let's talk about it," said Myrna, waving a dismissive hand. "That book has bought me no pleasure and much grief."

"What book is this?" asked Iris, ignoring her petition, and feigning ignorance.

Bud, for once, seemed eager to oblige them. "An early print of *Alice in Wonderland*," he sniffed, "a book for babies and women. Who in their right mind would waste their hard-earned money—or their husband's hard-earned money—on such a foolish thing?"

Myrna, apropos of nothing, said, "Abby, whatever happened to that young man you were seeing, the professor—Benjamin, I think his name was—"

"They severed contact," Bud broke in. "They haven't spoken since we started dating, have you, Abbers?"

Abigail twisted her hands uncomfortably. There was a peal of faint thunder, and a light rain began tapping at the windows.

"My goodness, a *first edition*," said Geneva, in her teacher's voice. "Now, would this be the handwritten early draft that Carroll wrote for Alice Liddell, *Alice's Adventures under Ground?* Or is it a first edition of the finished novel?"

Myrna looked mildly surprised that Geneva knew so much about the printing history of the *Alice* books. "The finished novel," she said, "from 1865. With Tenniel's pictures and such. The copy that I bought at auction was originally owned by Christina Rossetti and her brother, Dante. They were friends of Dodgson's, and he sent them signed copies. Both recalled being thoroughly enchanted by it."

"Did you learn that from the professor?" asked Bud with a desultory glare.

"Bud, don't be rude," said Abigail, her needles glinting in the lamplight.

Geneva had rather hoped that Myrna would offer to show them the novel, wherever it was hidden, but it seemed rude to ask; and when several minutes had elapsed, she began to feel they ought to be going. Myrna left the room and returned with an armful of inflatable child-sized floaties and life vests, which she threw down on the floor by the door leading out onto the back patio. Outside the rain was coming down hard now, making ripples in the swimming pool and mud puddles in the yard.

Iris had only just motioned to her belly to signal that she was getting hungry when Myrna turned round suddenly and said, "I have a terrible feeling about the wedding. I don't know if I want to go through with it. Do you think it's too late to call it off?"

Abby was so startled by this admission that she dropped the ball of yarn into her lap. "Mamaw," she said, "whatever for?"

Myrna balled her hands into tight fists. "I keep having the most horrible dream—blood in a swimming pool—and you and Bud and Jimbo all standing together in a graveyard—a funeral is taking place—but I'm nowhere to be seen. What's become of me? Why am I not there?"

Bud laughed a throaty laugh. "Anxiety dreams about getting old—is anyone surprised?"

But Myrna shook her head. "No, I've had those dreams. This wasn't one of those."

Bud smirked as if to say, "What then?"

"Mamaw," said Abby, face etched with concern, "if you're having second thoughts about marrying Jimbo—"

"Of course, I am," snapped Myrna. "I was married for nearly fifty-five years—and after all that time, to be sharing a bed with someone else—it feels like a betrayal of all we worked for. I can't walk down that aisle, knowing that his ghost will be standing among the guests, watching."

"You ought to tell Jimbo, then. Unless of course you think this is just pre-wedding jitters."

"I don't know what it is," said Myrna, sinking down into a rocking chair unhappily. "But I can't break off the wedding *now*, two weeks before the date. He would think it was something wrong with *him*. How would I explain to him—how could I ever hope to make him understand—"

"If you want," said Abby, reaching out and stroking her arm, "I'll tell him."

Myrna shrugged her away. "No, it has to be me."

"Then I'll be in the room when you do it. Or I'll be standing nearby, if you really think he'll be angry—if you think he might hurt you—Bud and I will be right there."

"No, no, he surely wouldn't hurt me. I don't know if you being there would help." Myrna wrung her hands. "I've been waking up in a cold sweat every night—just wave after wave of apprehension—and I don't know if it has anything to do with the wedding—but something strange and unavoidable is coming, and I'm frightened."

She seemed so agitated, in fact, that Abby thought it might be better if the visitors left so she and Bud could try to console her in private. They turned to go; though Geneva turned back at the door to say, "I hope we'll be seeing you again. I feel like we have so much to discuss, and we barely brushed the surface."

"Yes, I would like that," said Myrna, not even bothering to look up. "I've never met anyone who knew so much about, well, apart from Benjamin, of course—it was like having a friend."

Her voice trailed off. Abby laughed good-humoredly and said, "Bye, we'll be seeing you folks."

Iris opened the front door and together the three friends dashed through the rain and fog back to her car.

"Do we have to come back?" said Iris, as she was pulling out of the drive. "Those are just about the three most miserable people I've ever had the misfortune to meet."

"Brilliant, though," said George quietly. "The women, I mean. I'd like to have talked to them more."

Geneva said nothing. As the house slowly receded from view through a curtain of rain, she couldn't shake the feeling that she had just spoken to Myrna Nettles for the last time.

[5]

On Monday morning, Geneva herself was awoken from strange dreams by the buzzing of the phone on her bedside table. It was Gerry. Fumbling for her glasses, she said, "Hey, what's up?"

"Gen, were you friends with Myrna Nettles?"

"We met recently, yes." The phrasing of the question unsettled her, though in her groggy, half-awake state it took her a moment to figure out why. "What do you mean *were*?"

"Maybe you'd better come out here to her place."

An hour later, she was standing once again at the front of the Nettles' home. It was a quarter past eight. Stratus clouds hung low over the pines in a heavy, leaden sky. Iris, who had taken the morning off, stood rapping at the door in the hopes that someone—Abby, Jimbo, one of the policemen whose car was parked in the drove ahead of theirs—would open for them.

"Still doesn't seem real, does it?" she mused, when they had been waiting for about six minutes. "I feel like the door is going to open at any moment, and she'll be standing there, looking as lost and confused as ever, and it will have been one of those horrible misunderstandings that seems funny in retrospect—"

"I'll believe it when I see the body," said Geneva, though she felt an icy sensation of certainty in the pit of her stomach. It was no use asking *who would want to kill an eighty-two-year-old woman?* She had known willing murderers enough. Age was no barrier if the incentives were great enough.

"Perhaps we should've listened when she was going on about those horrible dreams," said Iris. "I got the feeling she was just being dramatic."

"She *was* being dramatic," said Geneva, feeling a light speckle of mist on her forearm. "She also happens to have been correct."

Iris knocked again, with no more success than before. They began to speculate about who might have done it. Iris thought maybe she had taken her own life, and that the whole story about the dreams had been a way of pointing suspicion toward someone else she had been hoping to frame for the killing as an act of revenge.

"That would be ingenious," said Geneva, "but Myrna never struck me as being a criminal mastermind."

"Maybe we never actually met Myrna," said Iris. "I saw an episode of *Poirot* where a man complains to Poirot that he's been having terrible dreams where he takes his own life... it turns out the man is impersonating someone else, whom he then murders—everyone assumes he died by his own hand—"

"You really think the Myrna we met on Saturday might have been an imposter?" said Geneva, shaking her head. "How do you account for the fact that neither Bud nor Abby made mention of the fact? Surely, they would have noticed?"

"Maybe they're in on it," said Iris, voice quivering melodramatically. "Maybe the real Myrna was gone for the weekend or—maybe she was already dead—"

Geneva never revealed how she felt about this new theory, for at that moment, the door opened to reveal Gerry. "Ah, glad to see the two of you finally made it," he said, as he stepped aside to let them through. His clothes were rumpled, as though they had been slept in; Geneva had a suspicion he had spent the night here. "If you make it to eighty-two without being murdered, one would think the rest of your life would be smooth sailing, but alas—"

"When was she found?" asked Geneva, following him into the living room.

"Yesterday, around noon. She had scheduled a pool party with five or six kids from church, ranging in age from six to twelve—but when her granddaughter, Abigail—"

"Yes, we met her just a couple days ago," said Iris. "In this very room, in fact."

"Of course, you did," said Gerry, looking only faintly surprised. "I won't even ask how you got tangled up with this lot. Abby drove straight over here after church to help finish setting up. She was feeling worried because Myrna hadn't come to church, which was apparently highly unusual for her —in thirty years, she only missed services once, on the weekend of her husband's death."

Geneva examined the living room in which Bud and Abby and the deceased had quarreled not two days before. It looked largely the same, except that someone had moved the floaties, and a pile of books that had been standing atop the coffee table had been relocated to a nearby shelf. The deer and elk heads glared balefully, as if wishing to speak of what they had witnessed. She shivered imperceptibly.

"She wasn't killed here."

Gerry gestured to the kitchen doors. "Abby found her floating face-down in the pool. At the present moment, it isn't clear whether she slipped in or was pushed in. We've released a statement saying it was an unfortunate accident—"

"But you don't believe that," said Geneva, "not for a minute."

Gerry's face remained expressionless. "I mean, do you?"

"Old ladies worth millions do have a strange habit of falling downstairs, or eating arsenic and kidney pie," said Iris. "I'd say it's more than suspicious. Surely someone was after her money."

"Yes, and I can't imagine anyone being *angry* enough at the old woman to want revenge," said Geneva. "Whatever the motive, this wasn't a crime of passion. No one cares about the elderly enough to hate them, sadly."

"She was getting remarried," said Gerry. "Clearly someone cared."

"I find that rather suspicious, too," said Iris, who had been staring at the fridge for some moments as if trying to gauge the morality of eating a dead person's foods. "If you tell me a millionaire in her sunset years is getting remarried, I'm going to guess that money was a factor."

"How much do we know about Jimbo?" said Geneva. "I've not met him."

"Haven't yet had the pleasure," said Gerry. "He seems like a decent sort, by all accounts—Abby encouraged the marriage because she knew her gran had been intensely lonely after the passing of her first husband, Roger or Rick or whomever—"

"I believe she said his name was Roy."

"But as I understand it," he added, "Myrna was having some second thoughts about getting married."

"I only know what she said to us on Saturday," said Geneva. "She'd been having terrible dreams. I got the feeling she was a little superstitious."

"Nothing to do with the character of the groom?" said Gerry.

"Not at all. Just a classic case of a woman about to undergo a major life change, which she was experiencing as a sort of apocalyptic event. It happens to people on the cusp of retirements, kids about to graduate from college—"

"She couldn't have guessed she was facing the ultimate apocalyptic event," said Gerry. "Death."

Geneva considered this. "I think she may have had an inkling, actually. It was Abby who suggested she was having wedding jitters. Myrna seemed to think her visions portended something darker and more ominous."

"Cassandra," said Iris.

The others turned to look at her.

"Well, it's the classic myth, isn't it? Cassandra was cursed by the gods to have premonitions of future disasters, but to be ignored when she tried to warn the Greeks what was coming."

"That's just being old, I'm afraid," said Geneva. "You say anything out of the ordinary, everyone thinks you're getting senile, having a *senior moment*, as they call it."

"One more thing to look forward to," said Iris dryly. "People already don't listen to me."

Gerry led them out onto the patio, waving to indicate the spot where Abby had found her grandmother's body. He recounted how she had made the discovery just as the first kids were arriving at the house from church—her frantic efforts to keep them from going into the backyard as she called the police—the mingled gasps of consternation and dismay as several of Myrna's old friends, who had come to assist, realized what had happened.

"When you're that old, you expect to die asleep in your bed. Even if she slipped, the sight of her floating there like a lotus petal must have been horrible for them."

Geneva preferred not to think about it. "Why didn't you call us yesterday?"

"Pardon?"

"I mean, why wait until this morning? I'd like to have seen the body, first thing."

Gerry strode to a glass-topped table near the kitchen window, on which had been laid a brown leather satchel. "I took pictures."

This didn't answer her question, but for the moment Geneva decided to let it go. "Show me."

Gerry hesitated. "You sure you wanna see this?"

Geneva gave him a look as if to say, "Don't patronize me."

Gerry shrugged and produced a sleek, silver digital camera, on which he had stored about a dozen photographs of Myra's body and the surrounding pool. He scrolled too quickly for the two women to get a proper look, but—apart from the corpse—Geneva didn't notice anything out of the ordinary. Her neck was a bit flushed and had assumed a ripe tangerine color like a summer sky at sunset; but there was no sign of a struggle. Not that she had expected any—at her age and weight, it would have been all too easy for someone a bit younger and with a bit more heft to sneak up behind and shove her into the pool.

The early morning clouds had dissipated, leaving a humid haze. Past the yard, at the edge of the woods, they heard a scuffling from the trees as of many hooves. Geneva began to feel uneasy, as if she was being closely watched by people or things unseen.

"Was anything stolen?" said Iris, into the long silence that followed. "Or, I guess, has anything gone missing?"

"Not that I'm aware of," said Gerry, returning the camera to the satchel with a puzzled expression. "Why?"

"There was a book—"

"Yes, the *Alice* book." His face colored slightly as he added, "I hadn't even considered that."

"You *what?*" cried two voices at once.

Gerry motioned for calm. "Listen, I'm running on about three hours of sleep—we searched the main rooms and the upstairs —nothing appeared to have been removed—but the book wasn't in any of those rooms, there's a secret panel in the wine cellar—"

"And have you gone down to the wine cellar since...?" Iris asked.

Gerry had the look Geneva had seen on some of her former students when they had forgotten to do an important assignment. In a quiet voice he said, "I'll be right back—you can either stay here or come with..."

But just then Geneva's phone buzzed in her shirt pocket. It was George. "Hang on, I need to take this."

"I'll go with him," said Iris, and jogged after Gerry back into the house.

Frowning slightly, Geneva accepted the call. "George? Hello?"

George's voice came loud but muffled, like a reporter in a rainstorm. "GENEVA? CAN YOU HEAR ME?"

"I can hear you just fine." said Geneva, pulling the phone from her ear. "Quiet down a little."

George didn't seem to hear her. "I'm at the pawnshop on Westbury and Elm—"

"George, I'm sorry, could this wait until I get home? I'm kind of in the middle of something—"

"Were you aware," he said, his voice lowering to normal range, "that Myrna Nettles—the woman we met not two days ago—had just died?"

"So I heard. I'm at her house right now."

George didn't show the least surprise at this. "Okay, well— like I said, I'm at the pawnshop—I like to come here on Mondays before my shift because they have a nice collection of paperback mysteries from the forties and fifties—anyway, there was a man in here not twenty minutes ago trying to pawn bed sheets that he claimed he had nicked *from Myrna's bed.*"

"*What?*" Geneva exclaimed.

"I wish I'd recorded the conversation on my phone. He and the man at the register, Tom Bowles, were chatting—Tom said, 'We don't get bed sheets of this quality every day,' and the man laughed and said they had come from the bed of an old lady, a millionaire several times over, who had just died—said he couldn't say more than that, as he was working for someone who had stripped her beds just hours after her death—said he'd be back tomorrow with some fine china—if I told you the amount of money Tom had given him for the sheets and the curtains—and then I saw on the *Bugle* website that Myrna had died, I was pretty sure she's the woman he was talking about."

He said all this in a breathless burst, like an old-time reporter broadcasting the news over the wireless. "George, you swear you're not pulling my leg?" said Geneva. "I really thought pawning bed sheets went out with the Victorians."

"Sure as I'm standing here, I saw them," said George emphatically. "We've gotta stake this place out tomorrow, you need to see this man—find out who he works for—"

"I'll handle it, George," said Geneva. "Thank you so much for telling me." Her attention had been drawn to a bright red button placed at the edge of the pool, jutting out of the concrete. She stared at it for a moment with a puzzled feeling. It reminded her of something, maybe a movie she had seen once, though she couldn't remember which...

"Love you, Georgie," she said absently. "I'll see you when we get home tonight."

She hung up the phone and was striding across the patio to examine the button more closely when she heard a noise behind her, past the wood fence at the front of the house— voices, a man and a woman's, raised in anger.

"You couldn't have shown up at a worse time," came a voice that was plainly Abby's. "I don't want to send you away, but you really shouldn't have come in the first place. If we're seen together—"

"I just need a few minutes of your time." It wasn't Bud's voice but someone else's—one she had heard very recently. "Give me three minutes, and I'll never bother you again. Promise."

"Ben, you don't have three minutes." said Abby, fear and anguish in her voice. "I'm not trying to get rid of you, but Bud is headed over. I've seen what he does to people—the power he has over them—"

"With the police here?" said Ben. "He's a bully, sure, but he's no magician."

But Abby was steadfast. "I'm not willing to take that chance. I'm only saying this because I love you."

Ben, however, was determined to have his say. "I know that he rules you with an iron fist—"

There was a slight pause, as though Abby had placed a hand over his mouth. "Not here," she said. "Not in front of the house."

A moment later, they walked past the open gate in the direction of the wood, Abby leading him by the hand. Geneva, still standing on the patio, immediately knew where she had seen him before. In his tweed jacket, patched at the elbows, and horn-rimmed glasses, he was unmistakable. She hesitated for a moment, debating whether she should follow. She didn't want to intrude on an intimate conversation, but if their discussion had bearing on the murder—

One thing was clear, though, Ben and Abby hadn't ceased seeing each other entirely since she had been cajoled into dating Bud. From the tone of her voice and her obvious concern for his safety, it sounded as though she still liked him. Bud must have sensed this, which may have accounted for his irritability and resentment. He had won the approval of Roy and Myrna, but Abby—though to all outward appearances meek and submissive—was inwardly drifting further and further. Only she had become adept at hiding the truth from herself, until Ben showed up and reminded her of the connection they had once had—a connection she and Bud lacked.

Setting her phone to silent and beginning to follow, Geneva had only just left the patio when the back door opened once more, and Iris came running out. She looked badly winded, as though she had just descended three flights of stairs.

"Gen," she said, "I've got good news and bad. Scratch that, no, it's all bad."

"What's up?" said Geneva, wondering if things could get any worse.

"The safe in the cellar has been opened. The book is gone. We know it was there a couple days ago, so it must have disappeared at around the time of the murder. But Gen— whoever stole it had the combination to the safe. She was killed by someone she knew and knew well."

[6]

"AND NOT ONLY THE BOOK," said Geneva as they stood together in the cold cellar, she and Iris and Gerry, "but curtains and bed sheets and expensive dishes, all of which you seem to have missed in your inventory of the house."

Gerry said nothing. He stood gazing into the depths of the open safe, as if hoping the book might suddenly reappear there.

"One question," said Iris. "How long did it take you to arrive at the house after the initial discovery of the body?"

"An hour and ten minutes," said Gerry. Geneva sucked in her breath. "Somebody thought it would be hilarious to leave a nail strip lying in the parking lot of the Whataburger, and I punctured two tires. Given that, I think I made pretty good time."

"And for all we know, she had already been dead for at least an hour—during which time any number of people could have gone in and out of the house." Geneva told them of the conversation George had overheard in the pawnshop.

Gerry let out an incredulous cough. "George just happened to overhear this? I'd like to see the odds on that."

"It's a small town," said Geneva. "Anyway, they'll be coming back tomorrow with more stolen goods. I'm guessing at around the same time. Iris, can you take another day off?"

Iris shook her head, but Gerry said, "If this is true and not just something our beloved George misheard—"

"What are you suggesting?" said Geneva.

"I want to handle this personally. Our guy committed any number of felonies entering the home of a dead woman and making off with her wares, potentially including murder. You three have been a huge help, pointing us in the right direction—"

"Don't condescend," said Geneva. "I want to be there when you nab this bloke. I have some questions I'd like to ask him."

Gerry considered this for a moment before saying, "I think maybe we can arrange that."

Nabbing him turned out to be easier than she had anticipated. George and Geneva returned to the pawn shop on the following morning at ten; he parked the car and they waited, eating their sausage-and-egg muffins and lightly toasted croissants. Twenty minutes later, a blue van pulled up in one of the empty spaces at the end of the lot. From it emerged a middle-aged man with thinning hair, wearing a t-shirt with a sketch of a grinning catfish on it. He was carrying a grey crate.

"That's him," said George, sitting up suddenly. "Shall we go in after him?"

"No," said Geneva, "we'll wait for him to come out."

They played Scrabble together via phone while they waited for him to come out. At ten past eleven, the doors opened, and he began heading back to the van. Geneva motioned for George to stay seated while she unbuckled herself and got out of the car.

"Beg pardon," she said to the man. "Can you help me? I'm looking for some rare books on the black market, and I was told you could help me."

Badly startled, the man set down his crate. He glanced around the parking lot as if to ensure they wouldn't be overheard. "Lady, I don't know what you're talking about," he said slowly. "I'm just making a delivery."

"Really, are you sure?" said Geneva. "Because I heard—"

She said no more, for at that moment two policemen with guns drawn came around a corner of the building. Within moments, the balding man had been handcuffed and placed into the back of a police car barely hidden behind a dumpster and some loose plastic palm fronds.

Twenty minutes of questioning at the precinct yielded the information that he had entered the Nettles' home on Sunday morning at eleven-thirty. "I wasn't aware that the lady was dead," said the man, whose name was Hugo Bartlett. "I'd been told eleven-thirty was the best time to visit because she and her girl would be at church."

"So this wasn't a personal visit," said Gerry. "You were working for someone."

"Ain't sayin,'" said Hugo.

"Legally," said Geneva, with no idea whether or not this was true, "you're in a lot less trouble if you were working on behalf of someone else."

Hugo considered this. "How much less trouble?"

Gerry regarded him coolly. "Years off your sentence," he said low.

"How many years?"

Gerry raised a significant brow. *"Years."*

Hugo asked for a pencil and a sheet of paper, on which he wrote a single name.

"Figs Hooperbag—I'm sorry, the man's name is Figs?" said Gerry. "I didn't know we were hosting any Hogwarts professors."

"He's a senior fitness expert," said Hugo, with a faint flush of relief, "and a *former* friend of Roy Nettles. They had a falling out—him and Roy and Myrna—shortly before the old man's death."

"Go on," said Geneva.

Hugo shrugged. "Roy and Myrna were very respected and influential people in the community. Figs thought he could use them to boost his failing business. He enlisted Myrna to promote it through her various networks—churches, gardening clubs and what-have-you. For a while it seemed to be working—attendance doubled, Figs was making more money than he could spend in a year. But then Myrna actually went and paid the place a visit."

"I'm guessing she wasn't a fan," said Geneva.

"You could say that," said Hugo. "Figs can be domineering—a reporter for the *Bugle* accused him of being a cult leader. His weight-loss methods are a little extreme. He yells. He once got in a woman's face because she had splurged on ice cream at her dog's birthday party. Myrna was livid, and she withdrew her endorsement. What's worse, she put out a statement urging people to seek other fitness centers. Now Hooperbags' is on the cusp of bankruptcy."

"And how did we get from there to you breaking into Bandersnatch Manor?" said Geneva.

"Figs needed the money," said Hugo, absently tapping his soda can, "and he wanted revenge. He enlisted me to break in and steal some of her things—nothing too big or fancy, just enough to keep him afloat for the next month or two. 'She's got so many dishes and cups and plates, she'll never even know if a few of 'em go missing,' is what he told me. 'Just grab what you can and get out before the old lady gets back from church.' I didn't realize she had stayed home. I didn't even know about the murder until later that night."

His drumming had been getting louder and louder; Geneva was tempted to reach over and take the can away from him. "Mr. Bartlett," she said, "when you went down into the cellar—"

"Pardon?" said Hugo.

"The wine cellar. To retrieve the book from the safe—"

Hugo motioned for a timeout. "Sorry, this is just a jumble of words to me. What book? What safe? Is there a secret stack of money hidden in some dank lair I should know about?"

Gerry searched his face. "You're not joking. You really don't have any clue what we're talking about."

"Look, I was given very specific instructions," said Hugo, his basset jowls quivering. "Go into the house, stick to the main rooms, clear out what you can, get out before church ends. Number one, I'm not a—what do you call 'em?—an expert at cracking open safes. Number two, I wouldn't have had the time. I was only there for about thirty minutes."

Gerry tapped on the tabletop, looking, for the first time in the interview, thoroughly flummoxed. "If he's telling the truth, admittedly a big *if,* you know what that means: there was at least one other person in the house yesterday. Both of them stole things—one of them stole an enormously expensive book —and one of them is a murderer."

"How long has this been going on?" asked Geneva.

She had found Abby in the boathouse down by the lake, rigging up one of the wooden dinghies. ("I like going out on the water sometimes," she had explained. "It's quiet out there. I like being alone with my thoughts.") With the water lapping in the distance, Geneva had recounted Hugo's arrest and the recovery of three crates full of stolen items from the pawnshop. Midway through the conversation, Abby's phone buzzed; from the despairing look on her face Geneva guessed it was either Bud or Ben.

Now Geneva repeated the question. Abby stared at her blankly.

"That's a rather vague question," she said at last, "but I assume you're referring to something you imagine is going on in my personal life."

"Well, I can see you're as smart as advertised," said Geneva dryly. "I'm referring to the fact that you've been dating one man while seeing another in secret. And that in a matter of weeks, you'll be marrying someone you have seemingly no interest in."

Abby merely smiled; she wasn't going to admit her real feelings so easily. "Bud has been the kindest person in the world to me," she said. "Roy and Mamaw both felt that he was the best person for me. Now that they're both dead, it would be a betrayal of their express wishes to break things off."

"Let's leave aside what they wanted for a minute." Geneva knelt down and reached for Abby's hands, which still grasped the rope. "It may surprise you to learn that we're no longer living in the Victorian era. You get a say in the choice of your partner."

Abby blinked back surprise, as if the idea of having personal agency was new to her. "You're maybe the fourth person to have said that. Ben's mother, Fancy—she's a chronic meddler —she's been trying her hardest to scuttle my relationship with Bud. She started a rather vicious rumor that I had been forced into the engagement against my will."

"Were you?"

Abby gazed down at the muddy ground. "She also wasn't too keen on Mamaw marrying Jimbo. Personally, I think she was a little jealous. Jimbo is closer to Fancy's age, and when we had our church jitterbug and ice cream social up at the house last August, I caught her flirting with him aggressively."

"Did you ever get the feeling that he reciprocated?"

Abby sank her fingers into the soft earth. "No. But then again, I never got the feeling that he liked Mamaw much, either."

Geneva was still trying to get a clear sense of their social network. "You said this woman, Fancy, is in her fifties or sixties—"

"Fifty-eight, I think—although she looks ten years older."

"I think I might have met her recently. Does she flirt with every man?"

"If there's even the remotest chance they'll flirt back," Abby replied. "And if they don't cooperate—"

She broke off, shivering slightly.

"What has she said about you?" asked Geneva.

"What *hasn't* she said?" said Abby. "She's launched whisper campaigns against both me and Mamaw. She said I was making out with some guy in the cry room at the back of the church, which wasn't true, but got me in a world of trouble with Bud—the only time he's ever hit me. She said Mamaw was getting old and could no longer be trusted to look after the children—when Mamaw was the most lucid woman of her age I've ever met."

"The children from church, you mean?"

Abby solemnly nodded. "Mamaw loved those children, they were the only reason she got out of bed in the morning. She would attend their little league games and cheer them on, show up to their fifth-grade graduations—and Fancy knew, she knew how much those relationships meant to Mamaw, which is why she had to go and try to destroy them." Abby was holding back sobs now. "So you get why Roy and Mamaw, and later Jimbo, were reluctant to let me go out with Ben. It wasn't Ben they objected to so much, it was his mother."

Geneva was beginning to feel an enormous welling up of sympathy for poor Abby, who seemed to have been inadvertently caught in the middle of an extended feud. By all accounts, her friendship with Ben had been perfectly lovely; but Fancy wasn't the sort of person to allow any sort of happiness to which she wasn't the chief party. "How does Ben feel about his mother's meddling and gossip?"

"He was a perfect gentleman about it," said Abby, with a small smile. "He asked her to stop, and when she refused, he cut off all contact. They're no longer on speaking terms. But it hasn't improved his position in this house; Mamaw and Jimbo are the sort of people who can never let go of a bad idea."

It was the closest she had come so far to admitting that she would rather not have been dating Bud. Given the casual nature of the slip, it was impossible to say whether she had intended it, or even noticed. Geneva thought it best not to press the issue. "Ben was hanging around the house on the day after the murder. Given your mamaw's dislike of him—"

Abby cut her off, looking deeply offended. "Ben would never have pushed that woman into a pool. He's the kindest, gentlest person—can barely ties his own shoes—a sort of Paddington Bear in human form."

He sounded, thought Geneva, like a younger version of George. It was hard to imagine anyone of that disposition committing a murder unless their situation was desperate. "And Bud—you say he hit you—"

"Only once," said Abby again. "And he didn't mean it. He apologized right after. It's what I deserved, anyway."

"First of all, no one deserves to be beaten," said Geneva firmly. "Second, if I remember correctly, Fancy was lying about you. He hit you because of a rumor that wasn't even true."

Abby looked as though she wanted to sink into the loam. "No, but I've had thoughts about Ben. I've been unfaithful in my heart to Bud, and he knows that. He knows I've daydreamed about being with someone else. He couldn't have hit me enough times to make up for that. He deserves to be with someone who loves him, and he got—me—"

She broke off. A shadow had appeared in the doorway, blocking out the light of the sun. Geneva glanced up. There stood a man in late middle age, wearing a pair of denim over-alls over a faded white tee, with a protruding belly, aviator sunglasses and the sort of mutton-chop sideburns that no respectable person had worn in over forty years.

"Abby," said the man, "I need you to come out here and feed the horses, I can't lift—" He paused, gazing suspiciously from the older woman to the younger. "Looks like y'all are havin' a pretty intense conversation. Anything I need to know about?"

"Nothing that concerns you, Mr. Clarin," said Abby. "Just two gals having a heart-to-heart."

The man, who had to be Jimbo, frowned. "Don't call me 'mister,'" he said, "every time you do it adds ten years to my life. Oh, and Abby? I'm gonna need your help tonight. I'm moving some of my stuff into the house—now that Myrna's gone, somebody needs to be on the property to keep an eye on things, make sure we don't have any more burglars. Call Bud and have him come over, will you?"

Abby nodded miserably but did not speak.

Jimbo looked hard at her. "You got somethin' you wanna say to me?" he asked.

Abby looked as though she had a great many things she wanted to say, but she shook her head.

"Didn't think so," said Jimbo, and he turned to leave.

$$[\ 7\ ]$$

"Here's what I don't get," said Geneva, when Iris picked her up that evening on her way home from work. The coroner's report had just come in, stating that Myrna had been killed by drowning when she slipped and fell into the pool. Gerry was preparing to declare the case officially closed. "I'm almost positive that she was drowned *by someone*—but then, how are there no traces on her body? No bruises?"

"I'm thinking it was like a panther attack," said Iris, slowing at the approach of a big truck. "All the murderer needed was a single, swift push—"

"But surely Myrna would have heard them coming."

"She was eighty-two," Iris pointed out. "She could barely hear *us*, and we were *yelling*. An elephant could have stomped into the yard, picked her up with its long truck and tossed her into the pool and she would have been none the wiser."

Geneva made a mental note to ask Abby about the state of her mamaw's hearing. "Myrna could swim, though. The church ladies said she spent more time in the pool than out of it. If someone tried to push her in, all it would accomplish is getting her a little wet."

"In which case they could say they were just having a laugh," said Iris, exiting the highway. "Youthful prank—muss up her hair a bit—no harm done."

"Except that in this case, harm *was* done," said Geneva. "She's dead."

"So...?"

"So pushing her into the pool wouldn't have done that. She must have been held down, by force, at some length, by someone considerably stronger. Held down until she died. My question is, how do you manage that without leaving any marks on the body?"

"I don't know," said Iris. "I've never tried to drown anybody, though I can think of several people who could use a good wash."

When they reached home, Iris prepared a quick dinner of chicken fried steak served over brown gravy, sautéed asparagus and golden tater tots, with ice cream in a mug for dessert. George offered to do the dishes, but Geneva told him to leave them in the sink and led the two friends to the communal swimming pool a few houses down which was completely empty. It was nearly seven; the sun was beginning its long decline, and over the fence they could hear the relentless whir of a leaf-blower.

"Here's what we're going to do," said Geneva, kneeling at the edge of the pool. "I'm going to sit here dipping my toes in the water, as I can easily imagine Myrna doing on a warm Sunday. Then the two of you are going to take turns sneaking up behind me and attempting to push my head into the water—"

"What?" cried Iris, aghast.

"But, and here's the crucial bit, *without leaving any physical trace.* If you leave so much as a thumbprint on my arm, you've failed. It's back to Murdering School with you. Who wants to go first?"

Neither George nor Iris wanted to go first.

"Gen, dear," said George, "I could never hurt you, not even for fun."

"Don't think of it as 'fun,' then," Geneva snapped. "Think of it as performing an experiment that will assist me in a criminal investigation."

"What if Mr. Leaf-Blower glances over here and sees me shoving your head under the water?" said Iris.

"Then Mr. Leaf-Blower needs to mind his own business," Geneva replied. "Come on, the day is waning fast."

Geneva took off her glasses and placed them at the edge of the pool. With a certain reluctance, Iris stepped forward and grabbed her arms, attempting to pin them behind her. Geneva gave all the resistance that a woman of eighty-two could have reasonably been expected to give, which is to say, not a great deal. Placing a hand at the base of her neck, Iris tried—far too gently—to push her down head-first into the water. She only succeeded in wetting the tip of Geneva's nose, for Geneva—largely on account of Iris's cooking—was far bulkier than the waifish Myrna.

"Sorry," said Iris, "I didn't want to set back the investigation by actually drowning you. How did I manage?"

"Too gentle and too rough," said Geneva, motioning to the bruises now forming on both arms. "Our murderer must have been a magician, because he seems to have drowned Myrna without laying a hand on her."

"Can I have a go at it?" asked George, and without any further warning he raced toward her across the sunlit concrete. Severely underestimating his own strength, he shoved her with all his might. Geneva, completely unprepared for the sudden attack, was flung headlong, in all her clothes, into the cold water.

An hour later, seated warming herself on the living room sofa with Marvin, the corgi, curled up at her heels, Geneva said, "It's a lucky thing I can swim—a very lucky thing."

"I've been thinking," said Iris, bringing her a mug of warm cocoa from the kitchen and setting it down on a little plate in front of her, "maybe we've been looking at it the wrong way."

"In what way?" said Geneva, reaching for the mug.

"I mean, all this time we've been working under the presumption that the murderer was targeting Myrna—whether for money or revenge. What if that's all wrong? What if the killer was trying to get back at the late Mr. Nettles for some perceived injury—and, well, since Mr. Nettles is dead, Myrna was dealt revenge in his stead?"

Geneva took a sip of her cocoa, thinking. "I think you might have something there. If it's a question of revenge, Myrna couldn't have had many foes—excepting Fancy, who loathed her with an inexplicable loathing. Roy, though... Roy was in business for many years. Roy would have made some enemies. Those enemies would have held grudges."

"Well, if there *was* a murder," said Iris, bringing in a bowl of Chex Mix, "we don't have much time to waste. Gerry doesn't seem too happy that we're still investigating, now that the case is all but closed."

"Gerry needs to have more faith in us," said Geneva. She had been treated to a half-hour-long lecture over the phone that afternoon about how she was "overstepping" her jurisdiction, and how it was a great privilege to assist the local police, one that could easily be withdrawn if she suddenly *went her own way.* "You know as well as I that Myrna Nettles didn't drown in four feet of water."

"Good luck proving it, though," said Iris. "We've searched every corner of that property, we've interviewed half a dozen suspects, and turned up exactly zero leads. We're no closer to finding the killer than we were on the day she died."

George, who had been seated in silent disgrace since shoving his girlfriend into the pool, leaned forward shyly. "I think we may have finally met our match here. A criminal who leaves no evidence whatsoever. The perfect crime."

Geneva kneaded her hands in frustration (she had been feeling annoyed with George ever since the incident at the pool). "No crime is unsolvable," she said. "We just haven't found the right clue yet—the key that will unlock the door into the garden—"

"And we may never," said Iris, tying her thick hair back. "If we so much as set foot on that property again, I've a feeling Jimbo will call the police—and then we'll both be in trouble."

"I think Abby would let us in, if it came to that," said Geneva, deep in thought. "Unfortunately, Abby's not in charge anymore... Jimbo has, rather quickly, taken over full control of the household. You should have seen him earlier, strutting about like the lord of the manor... acting like he had always owned the place..."

And judging from the look he had given Geneva as he left the boathouse, he hadn't been particularly fond of her, either... If they attempted to resume the investigation, he would be an impassable wall obstructing their way.

Not that such things had ever stopped her before...

"Let's go down the suspect list again," she said aloud. "See if there's anything we missed."

"Start with Fancy," said Iris. "The two of them had an ongoing feud. She personally sabotaged Myrna's reputation."

"Could she have drowned Myrna?" said Geneva. "No doubt the spirit was willing, but the flesh—she could have spent more time in the gym, to put it gently."

"How about Figs, then?" said Iris. "Former bodybuilder. Hired a man to break into Bandersnatch on the day of the murder—stole many things—"

"But not the expensive book, weirdly enough," said Geneva, tugging her robe close. "Assuming that Hugo was telling the truth, the safe was raided by someone else."

"Which raises the possibility that there were two thieves in the house at the same time, each unaware of the other's presence." There was a silence in which all parties tried to imagine the two thieves stumbling into each other. "Maybe Figs sent Hugo into the house, then secretly snuck in himself and stole the most valuable item, not wanting to entrust it to an underling."

"That's actually brilliant," said Geneva. She watched as George rose and strode across the room in the direction of the fireplace. "We know that Figs had a longstanding grudge against the late Mr. Nettles, which is what prompted the home-invasion-by-proxy. I get the impression that Roy was not always above-board in his business dealings—though I'm not sure Myrna had any clue about his ethical failings—"

"Which makes him the leading candidate," said Iris, as if listing off contestants on a game show. "Figs, I mean. He had the motive—he had the strength—he may have been inside the house at the time of the murder—"

"Let's not forget Bud," said George, who was, inexplicably, gathering old firewood and beginning to stack it in the fireplace. "A more odious, contemptible—"

"Odious, to be sure," said Iris, "but would he have killed the old woman? He didn't seem to have any particular beef with her—marrying into a rich family, he'd likely have wanted to keep her alive until after the wedding..."

Geneva, meanwhile, was watching George with a look of growing incredulity.

"George, dear," she said at last, as he began fumbling in his pockets for a lighter, "what in heaven's name has possessed you?"

George frowned an apologetic frown. "I feel—*bad*, frankly—that you're sitting there shivering because I heaved you into the cold waters. I thought maybe if I got a fire going, it could help you to warm up faster."

"Are we really lighting a fire?" said Iris with a bemused air. "Hilda and the other neighbors are going to think we're quite mad."

Geneva let out a sharp exclamation of surprise. George and Iris both turned round at once.

"Are you having a stroke?" said Iris.

Geneva shook her head. "No, I'm perfectly fine, I... I just remembered something..."

"Well, don't leave us hanging. What was it?"

Geneva didn't answer for a long moment. She couldn't believe she had been so foolish as to overlook such a vital clue —one that had been staring her in the face since the moment of her arrival at Bandersnatch.

"Last Saturday," she said, "when we drove up to see Myrna— did you notice anything particularly strange about the game-keeper's cabin?"

"Not that I can recall," said George, running a hand through his thinning hair. "I remember thinking it looked like Hagrid's hut, standing at the edge of the forest with the chimney emitting those cheerful puffs—oh...."

For George had suddenly seen precisely what Geneva was getting at.

"Answer me this," said Geneva, sitting forward on the sofa: "Why would a gamekeeper have a fire going *in the middle of May?* On a day when it was pushing ninety degrees in the shade?"

No one could think of a good answer to this. But then Iris said—

"You don't light a fire to get warm, not in the middle of spring
—you light it if you're trying to get rid of something."

"What sort of something?" asked George, plainly puzzled.

"Important records, files, any number of things," Iris replied.
"How many Agatha Christies hinged on a will or a letter
being wholly or partially burned in the fireplace?"

Geneva had already risen and was heading for the stairs. "I
know that look," Iris added. "Where are you headed?"

"To get ready to go out," Geneva called from the top of the
stairs. "Someone was in the cabin that day—someone other
than the gamekeeper, I'm willing to bet—and if we can learn
what they were trying to get rid of, I suspect we'll know who
killed Myrna Nettles."

[8]

THEY LEFT the station wagon parked at the front of the drive within a dense copse of trees overgrown with violets and Creeping Charlie. George was crestfallen when Geneva asked him to stay behind and look after the car.

"We need to head up there on foot because I don't want to risk us being seen," she explained. "For the moment, no one needs to know we're here. But I also don't want our car getting stolen. Is your phone charged?"

George, still looking offended, nodded weakly.

"Good. Keep a sharp eye out—if I suddenly text you the word DOLLY in all caps, you need to call the police. Don't text, don't try to call me, don't come running up the drive trying to find us—"

"Why not just call the police now?"

"Because it wouldn't leave us enough time." She smiled sadly at him, feeling a twinge of guilt for how she had been treating him for most of the evening. There was a greater than zero chance that they were looking at one another for the last time. "I'm sorry I fussed at you about the pool."

"Don't be," said George with a stoic air. "That's what I do, I mess things up. It's what I'm best at."

"Maybe sometimes. But I still think you're fantastic."

She turned to leave, Iris following a pace or two behind. She continued to feel George's eyes on her for some time as they emerged from the copse and began jogging along the curve of the drive, keeping some distance from the road to avoid being spotted by passing cars.

"'Need him to guard the car' my foot," said Iris once they were out of earshot. "Any and all thieves are welcome to it."

"I needed to give him some kind of assignment," said Geneva, "so he wouldn't feel excluded. But I also didn't want him accidentally getting in our way tonight."

They hurried on their way. It was almost nine and the last sliver of sunlight was fading over the firs. Iris had brought a flashlight from the car, which they used to navigate the dense tangles and shrubs. Once or twice, Geneva had to stop and extricate her cardigan from a low-hanging birch limb or a patch of bramble. A bit further on, they came upon a series of rivulets cutting through the wood in a checkerboard formation, making the ground damp and muddy. Iris swore under her breath as she inadvertently stepped down into the water, soaking her socks up to the ankles.

"I'm plum tuckered out, as the kids say," said Iris, looking badly winded. "That drive seemed a lot shorter when we drove up on Saturday. How did folk get anywhere in the days before petrol?"

They rounded the final corner and Myrna's old home—the home that Jimbo had now unceremoniously taken over—came into view. On the broad lawn at a distance of about fifty yards from the house stood the gamekeeper's cabin, front-facing windows cheerfully lit. In the paddock a bit further back, the horses stamped and whiffled, looking restless.

"No idea how this is going to go," said Geneva as they neared the cabin. "The staff may have felt a loyalty to keep Myrna's secrets—but they may not feel that loyalty for a new employer."

"Honestly," said Iris, "I think your best bet is to text Abby and let her know we're here. She'll be able to get in touch with anyone we need to interview and explain the situation. She's lived here long enough that I think the staff probably trusts her."

"There's just one problem, though," said Geneva: "I don't know if we can trust Abby."

They walked on in silence for another ten minutes, sticking close to the more shadowy corners of the property. Reaching the cabin at the woods' edge, Geneva climbed the stoop and knocked twice at the front door. From within they heard the shutting off of a television and the low putter of approaching footsteps.

"Hello?" came a woman's voice after a long pause. "Who's there?"

The door opened to reveal a stout, middle-aged woman in a brown skirt and a purple wool sweater, with a shawl draped across her shoulders. She peered at them narrowly from behind her large, wire-rimmed glasses, which only half-concealed the tattoo of a dolphin over her right eye.

"Sorry, if you're looking for Abby—"

"We're not looking for Abby," said Geneva, "not yet. We're private detectives, and we'd like to have a word about some things that may have happened here over the weekend."

The woman hesitated for a moment, looking conflicted. There was an old-fashioned dial phone hanging on the wall just within reach of the door. "I have orders, you know," she said. "That if two women were ever to come nosing around here, I'm to phone the house immediately."

"I'm quite sure that you do," said Geneva calmly.

The woman drew in a deep breath, and all her resolve seemed to give way. "But I reckon what Mr. Clarin don't know, won't hurt him." To Geneva's immense relief she stepped aside, motioning for them to enter the cabin. "If he catches us here talking, that'll be the end of my job, but—well, it's really not worth staying now that Myrna has passed on, is it?"

"You might find reason to stay," said Geneva. "You could look after Abby, Miss—"

"Tolliver," said the woman, bustling toward the kitchen, "and I'm afraid Abby is going to be beyond my help before very long, if she isn't already. The thought of her marrying that horrible man—who's done nothing but berate and antagonize —those that knew her best always felt Ben was the one for her, and I think Myrna was coming around—"

"Her death was rather conveniently timed, no?" said Iris.

Ms. Tolliver froze and peered up at them from behind the fridge door. "Oh, my dears," she said low. "You don't know the half of it."

Geneva waited, expecting her to go on. Instead, hands trembling, Ms. Tolliver reached for a spray bottle that stood on the counter. A row of potted plants stood against the sink, their tendrils trailing. Realizing that she had grabbed the wrong bottle, Geneva said, "Wait."

Ms. Tolliver paused, looking a little lost.

"Sorry, I think you may have gotten your sprays mixed up," said Geneva gently. "Unless you were intending to douse your plants with Lysol and ammonia."

Ms. Tolliver looked from her to the bottle. "Don't mind me," she said, plainly troubled, "just feeling a bit overwhelmed lately... I suppose I should start packing up my things, I can't imagine I'll be here for much longer..."

She went on muttering to herself as she rummaged noisily beneath the sink for the plant mister. Iris and Geneva, however, were keen to bring her back around to the original topic of discussion. "I'm sorry, what don't we know the half of?" said Iris.

Ms. Tolliver dropped a cast-iron skillet.

"No, there's no use getting into it," she said. "It's more than my job's worth—"

"You just said you're planning on leaving," said Geneva. "What's the use of keeping secrets at this juncture? It can't matter that much to you."

"Don't be naïve," she replied, with sudden aggression. "You've been in this business long enough, you ought to have learned by now that there are people you simply don't cross—not if you value your freedom—"

"You could help us to put those people away," said Geneva, "so they can't hurt you."

Ms. Tolliver shook her head. Geneva felt keenly that something was wrong; she wasn't looking them in the face, and her studied evasiveness was getting more and more disconcerting.

"There was someone here," said Iris, "on Saturday. There was a fire in the chimney—something was burned—"

The woman rose to her feet; even at her full height she barely reached Iris's chest. She held fast to the cabinet door, as if struggling to maintain her center of balance.

"When Myrna and Jimbo were first engaged," she finally said, "Myrna revised the terms of her will leaving him full control of the estate and her wealth in the event of her death. But then I think lately she was having second thoughts... she kept going on about these dreadful dreams she was having—"

"Yes, she mentioned those," said Geneva.

"Well anyway, a few weeks back, she wrote a second will in secret. Legally the terms of this will could only be disclosed after her death. Not even Jimbo knew about it. No one knew about it except her and her solicitor and the two witnesses, of whom I was one."

She hesitated.

"Go on," said Geneva.

"Myrna had made up her mind," she said, "that Abby was going to be her heir. She loved Jimbo, but she knew him well enough by now to know that he couldn't be trusted. She also knew—and this is a secret that she had been keeping for twenty-five years—that Abby was not her legal granddaughter. She had taken custody of the girl after her mother's death in a car accident in 1989; the woman had been an old friend. But Abby had never been formally adopted; I'm not even sure she knows all this. Myrna, however, was making plans to finalize the adoption and leave her the inheritance."

This was a great deal of information to take in at once, and it considerably changed Geneva's understanding of the dynamics within the family. "So Jimbo, her own fiancé—"

"... had been removed from the will, yes. And Abby was set to inherit, though she didn't know it. Before this could happen, though, Myrna wanted to sit down and have a conversation with Abby about the fact that they weren't related by blood— a conversation that they never managed to have before her death. Abby knows of the accident but has grown up believing that her mother was Myrna's daughter."

"But surely the lack of pictures—"

"There were pictures of Abby's mom in the house," said Ms. Tolliver. "Myrna made sure of that. She... misled Abby as to the nature of her relationship with her mother. I think she always intended to tell her the truth eventually, but as she grew older it became harder and harder. She kept putting it off."

"Right, I think I'm following," said Iris. "But that still doesn't answer her question—who was in this cabin on Saturday? What were they trying to get rid of?"

"Oh, as to that," said Ms. Tolliver, very quietly, and with a nod of her head to the door behind them, "I'm afraid you'll have to ask him."

They turned round. Jimbo had slipped silently into the room while Ms. Tolliver had been telling her story, and he stood in the doorway holding a pistol in one hand. His double chins now bore a three-day's growth of beard, as though he had been too busy arranging the funeral to attempt looking presentable.

"Thank you, Sarah," said Jimbo. "You did the right thing by texting me."

Geneva threw a stony glare at Ms. Tolliver, who blushed apologetically.

"And in answer to your question," he added, keeping the pistol aimed squarely in Geneva's direction, "the old lady severely misjudged her ability to keep a secret. All the staff gossip. It was only a matter of time before I learned of the new will—and I did what any self-respecting man would have done in the same circumstances. I acted in my own interest."

"You burned the will," said Iris.

Jimbo nodded, looking rather pleased with himself. "And the adoption papers, which she had so foolishly left here in the hopes I wouldn't stumble across them—she knew I had the combination to the safe, I could open it whenever I wanted—"

He stepped forward a few paces, keeping the gun steady. "I suppose this makes me the baddie. Very well, go on and think that if you'd like. Frankly the judgment of prim, middle-aged women never concerned me much. I was owed a great deal of money, and she tried to deceive me by taking that money away from me and then hiding the fact. I don't see how I did anything wrong."

"There's the small matter of you having killed Myrna," Geneva pointed out.

"Yes, that was ethically problematic," said Jimbo, "but again, it couldn't be helped."

"Ethically *problematic?*" cried Iris, aghast.

"I mean, put yourself in my position. The old woman had, at most, two or three years left—years of increasing misery and discomfort, old friends dying, hair falling out, what was left of her memory fading. One might argue that I did the loving thing by bringing her existence to an abrupt and merciful end. If there's a heaven—" here he gripped his throat, looking strangely constricted, as if afflicted by a momentary seizure— "if there's a heaven, she will have already forgiven me for it."

Geneva's phone was now buzzing, but she didn't dare reach for it. If he turned away for even a second, she could text George and warn him... but his eyes had remained rigidly fixed on hers since the moment he entered the cabin. She could only pray that George had sensed their delay and acted accordingly.

"How did you do it?" she asked, in an effort to stall him.

"Much like anything else," said Jimbo, "with great care and planning. I waited until she was standing outside by the pool getting the water ready. The kids would be arriving within the hour, so I had to act quickly, but I knew what had to be done—I'd been rehearsing the deed in my head for weeks, so that when the moment came, I acted on brute instinct. It was like slow walking through a dream I'd had many times. I took a throw pillow from the sofa and, coming up behind, placed it squarely on the back of her head and forced her face down into the pool. She struggled a bit, those little arms flailing, but gave up after a moment or two. There wasn't much fight left in her. I think she wanted to go."

"I'm sure it's very comforting to think so," said Iris, glowering at the man with undisguised contempt.

"Well, like I said, I never wanted to kill her." He raised the pistol slightly. "Any more than I want to kill you."

They had come to the pivotal moment. If Geneva and Iris were going to leave the cabin alive, they would have to appeal to whatever was left of his conscience.

"Look, you killed an old lady," said Iris. "I won't sugarcoat it, that's really bad. But you don't have to compound the mistake by killing *us*. One murder on your résumé is bad enough."

"So said the lamb," said Jimbo with an unconcerned air, "right before she was pounced upon and eaten by the lion."

Geneva, guided more by instinct than thought, reached for the nearest thing to hand—the spray bottle standing on the kitchen counter. With a single deft motion, she sprayed the fluid into Jimbo's face. Jimbo let out a loud, anguished cry and pressed his palms to his eyes, dropping the gun on the tiled floor.

"That was the plant mister, right?" said Iris. "Please tell me you sprayed him with the plant mister."

"I think? I'm pretty sure?" Geneva held up the bottle, which read *Windex Powerized Glass Cleaner with Ammonia D.* "Er, sorry about that," she added, realizing why his reaction had been so intense and dramatic. "On the bright side, your eyes probably won't fall out."

"Too bad," said Iris, stooping to pick up the gun, amidst Jimbo's yelping. "Now I may never know what a weird old murderer looks like with no eyes."

"Be a shame to have to spray you again," Geneva said to the writhing man. "Luckily I think I hear the police outside."

[9]

Completely disregarding Geneva's orders, George had phoned the police when they had failed to return after twenty minutes. He met Gerry at the front of the drive and rode along in the back of the car to the cabin, where he emerged to greet the women as Jimbo came stumbling from the house with his hands raised.

"Sorry, I never learned to follow orders," said George, wrapping Geneva in a tight hug.

"I hope you never do," said Geneva, and they held each other for a long moment as the horses whickered in the paddocks behind them.

Once they had disentangled, and after the two women had given a full report to the police about the events of the past half hour (only omitting Ms. Tolliver's role in drawing Jimbo to the cabin), Iris felt that they ought to go find Abby, to ensure she hadn't come to any harm.

As they crossed the broad, dew-soaked lawn Geneva texted her to let her know that they were on their way to the house. "Also, I have some news that you might be intrigued to hear. We'll talk in a minute."

But Abby didn't respond. Finding the front door unlocked, they spent a couple minutes debating the ethics of entering someone's home before Geneva pushed past Iris and strode in. Abby was not in any of the main rooms, nor—so far as they could tell—in her bedroom, which she had been in the process of vacating, but finally George found her downstairs, trapped in the wine cellar like Fortunato and banging for someone to let her out.

"Did Jimbo trap you in here?" asked Geneva, as they led her upstairs into the brightly lit kitchen.

Abby laughed. "Goodness, no—I accidentally trapped myself. There's a key to the upstairs and I forgot to bring it with me when I went down there to search through some of Mamaw's old records. I figured it wouldn't be a problem so long as I just left the door open, but then there came a slight gust of wind and it slammed shut."

"Brilliant," said Geneva. "I guess it's lucky we came by."

"Yes, because I didn't bring my phone. I'm a wee bit clumsy and forgetful, sometimes—like one of those air-headed young women in a Dickens novel."

"George can relate," said Iris, "can't you, George?"

George nodded meekly; he had once locked himself in his own car and it had taken a professional locksmith an hour to get him out.

Abby brought out the snack trays that she had bought for Sunday's party, and they sat around the kitchen table eating carrots and celery and beef summer sausage and Provolone slices whilst Geneva and Iris took turns recounting the events leading up to the arrest of Jimbo, and the revelation that Mamaw hadn't been Abby's real grandmother—a revelation that Abby received with a certain level of hurt and disappointment.

"Well, for all intents and purposes, she *was* my mamaw," she said, once the initial shock had subsided. "She raised me— brought me up by hand—would have made me heir to her fortune if—" She paused just long enough for them all to reflect that there was no surviving copy of the revised will. "And I don't care about the money, especially—but I would like to have known who my real mother was—and the only person who could have told me is dead."

Geneva reached for her hand across the table. She was reminded of that line from Shakespeare, uttered by someone who had just received equally life-altering news: *Such welcome and unwelcome things at once 'tis hard to reconcile...*

George rose suddenly. His attention had been captured by a silver-framed portrait on the marble counter.

"Who is this?" he asked softly. "Do—did you know this woman?"

Abby nodded. "That was my mom, or so I've been told. Taken just a few days before she died. It might be the last picture she ever took. Myrna rescued it from her house shortly after her death, along with me."

George gazed at the picture for a long moment, seemingly lost in thought.

"I knew her, too," he said at last, very quietly. "I called her Irene, but her real name was Katie. We dated for about a year, back in 1987. She... she was everything. Probably the best woman I've ever had the fortune of knowing."

Geneva looked pensive, but before she could speak, Iris raised one hand and pointed it, with a perplexed look, from George to Abby. She said in a low voice, to Geneva, "Should we...?"

"Yeah, I think we had better clear out," said Geneva, already rising. "We're going to take a turn about the grounds. George, why don't you stay here? I think you'll find that you and Abby have much to catch up on."

They left George and Abby in the kitchen, gazing in confusion and growing understanding at one another, and emerged from the house onto the cool, breezy lawn.

"Okay, so here's what I'm wondering," said Iris, as they skirted the perimeter of a stone fountain and waded out into the moonlit grass. "Who was that woman—the woman who tried to tell us?"

"Friend of Myrna's, I'm guessing," said Geneva. "She couldn't have kept that secret her whole life—not in a town of this size. There would have been people who knew. I'm surprised no one ever told Abby."

"Sometimes the person in question is the last to know," said Iris sadly. "I knew a woman who had an identical twin and didn't find out until well into her middle age. Her mother had managed to keep the secret for fifty years."

Midway between the house and the paddocks, there stood a gazebo hedged round with flowerbeds in which Myrna had planted hollyhock, daylily and Black-eyed Susan. Geneva was no expert in inheritance law, but she couldn't help feeling that the property would find its way into Abby's hands. Certainly, Jimbo would never live here, and there was some comfort in that. Pausing near the wood steps, she gazed up at a night sky spangled with a thousand stars.

"If George was going to have a daughter," she said after a pause, "I guess I'm glad it's Abby. There were clues all along the way, now that I think about it. Their shared clumsiness. Their love of literature. Their mutual fixation on the Beatles."

"The apple has not fallen far," said Iris. "It's funny—he didn't even raise her, and yet she managed to turn out just like him. And the fact that we happened to stumble into her life in this way... it's enough to make even a cynic like Bud believe in some grand design."

Geneva shook her head. "I'm afraid Bud wouldn't believe it, even if the gazebo suddenly acquired a mouth and started singing, 'Auld Lang Syne.'"

"I feel like we've seen at least one miracle tonight."

Geneva stood silent, reflecting. Somewhere in the deep woods she heard the hiss of a critter. At almost the same instant, a barn owl went gliding under the moon like a balsa-wood plane. It came to rest on a bare branch at the edge of the property, its dark eyes glittering peckishly in the moonlight.

"Maybe," she said at last. "Or maybe the miracle is continuous and ongoing, and there are nights when our eyes are opened."

"Maybe someday you can explain to me what that means in English," said Iris, offering her arm. "Shall we go look at the horses?"

Geneva nodded eagerly. Together they left the gazebo and continued on their way up the flower-strewn esplanade.

The End

CONTINUE READING...

THANK you for reading **_Two Sleuths & A Swimming Pool!_ Are you wondering what to read next?** Why not read **_Sisters & Switchery?_ Here's a sneak peek for you:**

It was a cold Saturday in early March, and nobody was feeling particularly happy. George Wilson had come over that morning excitedly brandishing the DVD for John Carpenter's *The Thing,* a horror movie about a team of scientists trapped in a polar research station with a shape-shifting alien. The movie hadn't met with the reception he was expecting: his lady friend, Geneva Pomolo, had pulled out her phone and started answering emails during the gory bits, while her housemate, Iris Reeves, had gotten up about midway through and gone to the kitchen in search of snacks. She had never come back.

A disgruntled silence fell once the movie had finished. Iris returned as the credits were rolling, cheerfully carrying a plate of lemon bars. George sat sulkily on the sofa, awaiting Geneva's reaction.

"George, I don't know what to tell you," she said finally, setting her phone down. "That was quite a bit more gruesome than your typical episode of *Endeavour*."

"You mean you didn't like it?" George asked sadly.

"Was I supposed to like it? There's a scene where a giant mouth appeared inside a man's chest and chomped off another man's arms."

"Wow, I'm actually kind of sorry I missed that," said Iris.

George hadn't yet given up hope that he could bring them around to liking the movie. He had the air of a preacher harping on one of his favorite texts. "You have to admire those special effects, though. Entirely practical, made in 1981 without the benefit of CG—"

"Somehow that makes it worse," said Geneva. "The effects were so good it made the movie that much harder to watch. It was disgusting."

"But the gore didn't overwhelm the movie," said George, trying another tack. "This isn't your average horror film, all blood and jump scares. It's that feeling of isolation, of suspicion—of being trapped in the snow with a killer on the loose, like in *Murder on the Orient Express*—"

"Why couldn't we have just watched that?" Geneva replied.

George threw up his hands in defeat. "I really don't get the both of you," he said. "I just showed you one of the greatest horror films of all time, some would say the greatest, and you have no appreciation for the talent, the level of craftsmanship on display—"

Click Here to Continue Reading!

https://ticahousepublishing.com/cozy-mystery.html

Donna Muse has been a mystery buff for years! But she hasn't been a fan of blood and gore. So when the Cozy Mystery genre came into being, she jumped on board with both feet. She loves the amateur sleuth and is fascinated by the intense and often comical way the perpetrator is revealed. Donna lives in Maine with her husband, loves walking by the surf, fishing for striped bass, and playing with her grandchildren and her cats.

contact@ticahousepublishing.com